LITTLE SCHOLARZ

Cursive
WRITING BOOK

Capital and small letters

NAME ____________________________

CLASS _____________SEC._______

SCHOOL ________________________

____

LITTLE SCHOLARZ PVT. LTD.

A for Apple

🖌 Trace and write:

Date: ....   Teacher's signature: ....

a for aeroplane

Trace and write:

Date: 3   Teacher's signature: ....

 B for Balloon

🖐 Trace and write:

Date: ....

Teacher's signature: ....

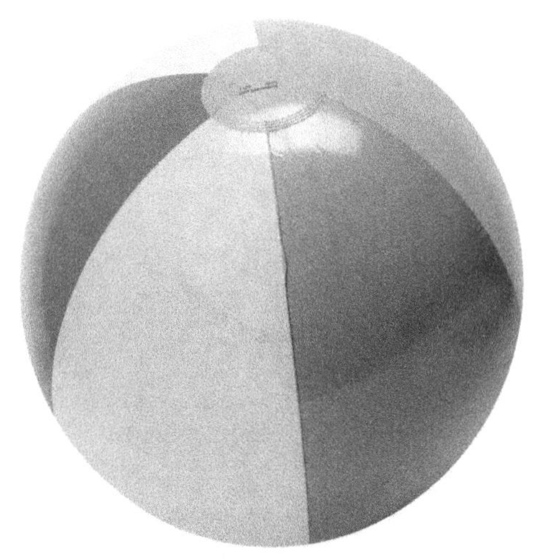

b for ball

Trace and write:

b b b b b b b b b b

b b b b b

b b b b b

b b b

b b

b

Date: ....

Teacher's signature: ....

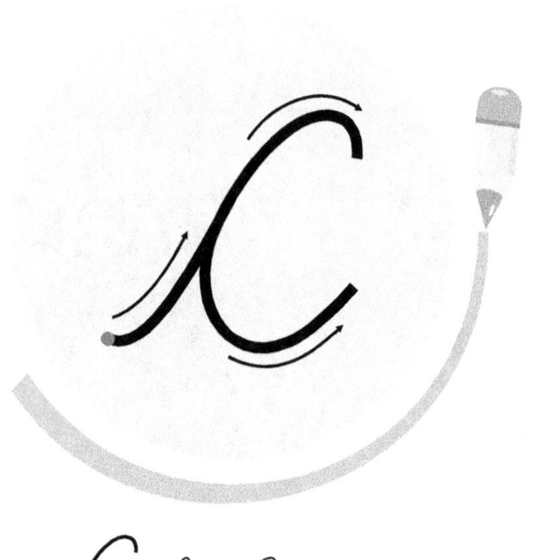

$\mathcal{C}$ for Cat

Trace and write:

$\mathcal{C}$ $\mathcal{C}$ $\mathcal{C}$ $\mathcal{C}$ $\mathcal{C}$ $\mathcal{C}$ $\mathcal{C}$ $\mathcal{C}$ $\mathcal{C}$ $\mathcal{C}$

Date: ....

Teacher's signature: ....

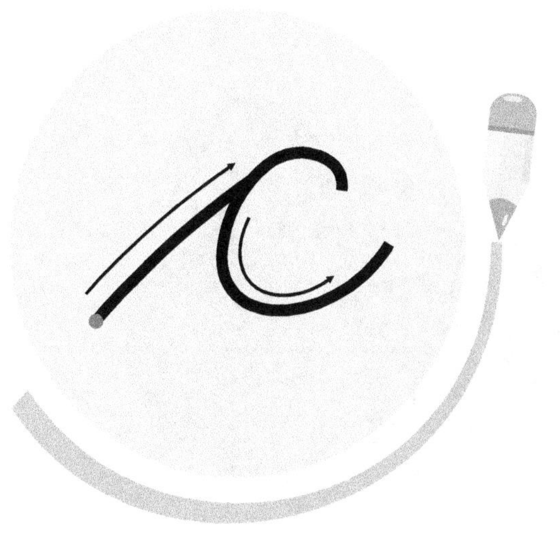

C for cake

🖐Trace and write:

Date: ....

Teacher's signature: ....

$\mathcal{D}$ for Duck

🦆 Trace and write:

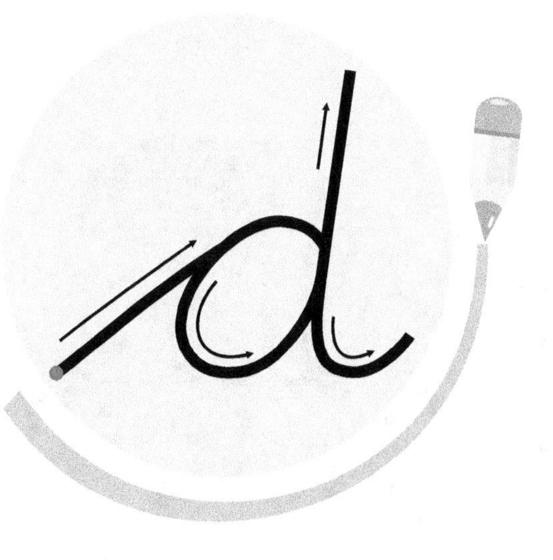

d for doll

Trace and write:

d d d d d d d d d d d d

d d d d d

d d d d

d d d

d d

d

Date: ....   Teacher's signature: ....

Trace and write:

e for elephant

🖐 Trace and write:

Date: ....

Teacher's signature: ....

F for Fish

Trace and write:

Date: ....

Teacher's signature: ....

f for frog

Trace and write:

Date: ....

Teacher's signature: ....

G for Goat

Trace and write:

G G G G G G G G G G G G G G G G G G G

G G G G G

G G G G

G G G

G G

G

Date: ....   Teacher's signature: ....

g for grapes ____

🖊 Trace and write:

| g | g | g | g | g | g | g | g | g | g |

Date: ....

Teacher's signature: ....

H for Hat

Trace and write:

Date: ....

Teacher's signature: ....

h _for hen_

🖐 Trace and write:

Date: ....

Teacher's signature: ....

I for Ice cream

🦋 Trace and write:

Date: ....   Teacher's signature: ....

🦋 Trace and write:

| *i* | *i* | *i* | *i* | *i* | *i* | *i* | *i* | *i* | *i* |

Date: ....   Teacher's signature: ....

J for Joker

Trace and write:

Trace and write:

Date: ....

Teacher's signature: ....

$\mathcal{K}$ for Kite

🦋 Trace and write:

$\mathcal{K}$ $\mathcal{K}$ $\mathcal{K}$ $\mathcal{K}$ $\mathcal{K}$ $\mathcal{K}$ $\mathcal{K}$ $\mathcal{K}$ $\mathcal{K}$ $\mathcal{K}$ $\mathcal{K}$

Date: ....

Teacher's signature: ....

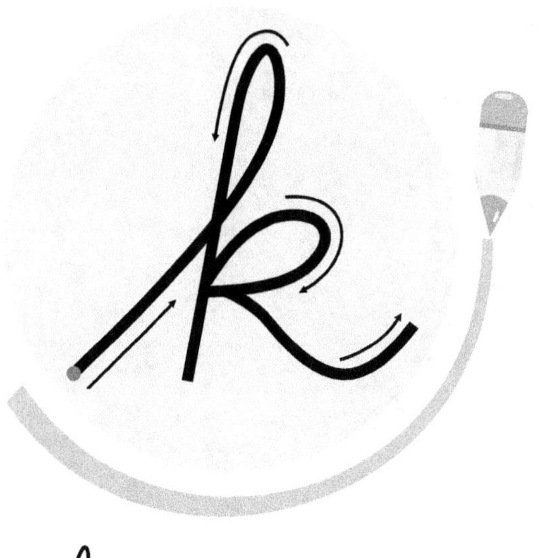

k for kettle

k k k k k k k k k k

k k k k k

k k k k

k k k

k k

k

Date: ....

Teacher's signature: ....

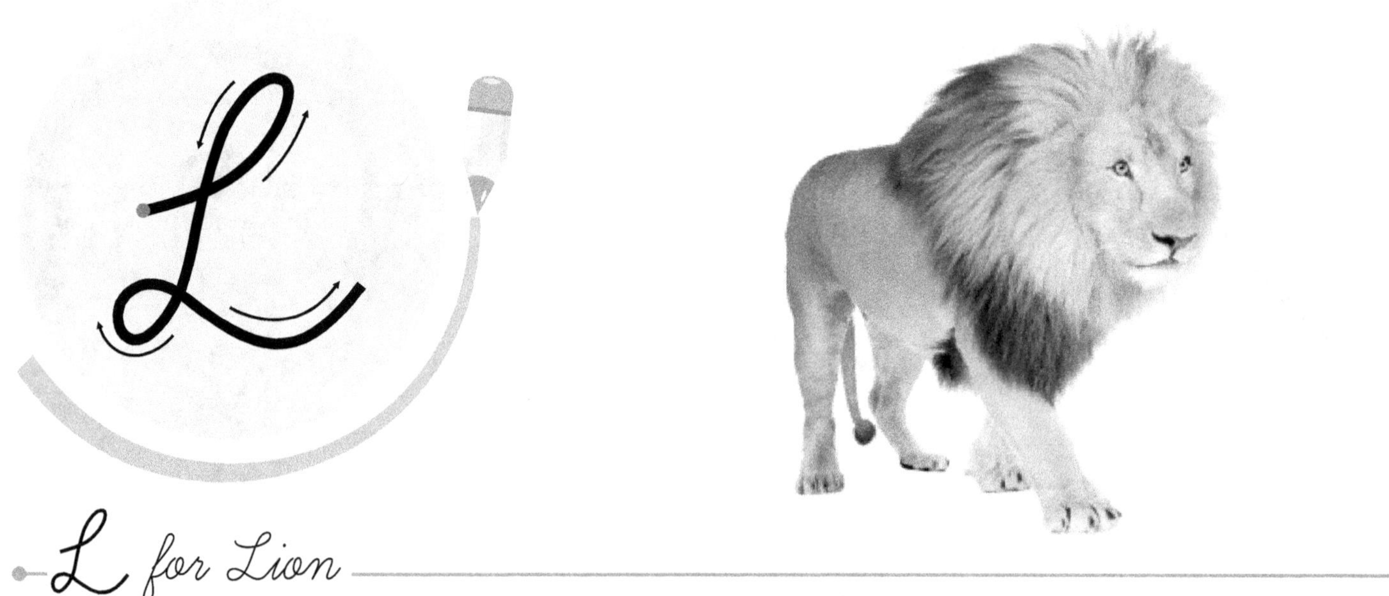

$\mathcal{L}$ for Lion

🖊 Trace and write:

Trace and write:

Date: ....

Teacher's signature: ....

$\mathcal{M}$ for Mango

m for mug

m m m m m m m m m m

m m m m m

m m m m

m m m

m m

m

Date: ....

Teacher's signature: ....

$\mathcal{N}$ *for Nest*

☙ Trace and write:

$\mathcal{N}$ $\mathcal{N}$ $\mathcal{N}$ $\mathcal{N}$ $\mathcal{N}$ $\mathcal{N}$ $\mathcal{N}$ $\mathcal{N}$ $\mathcal{N}$ $\mathcal{N}$

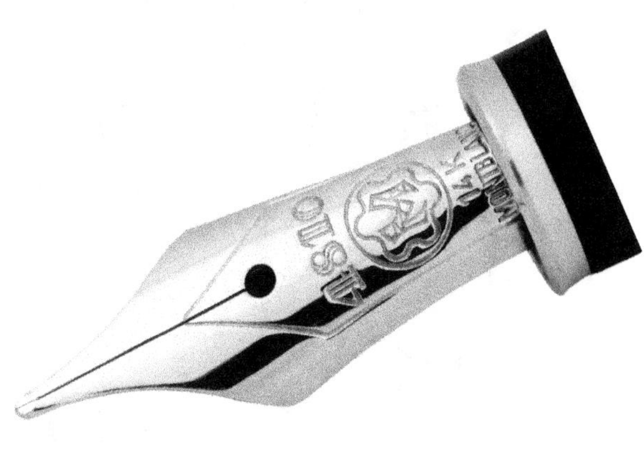

$\mathscr{n}$ for nib

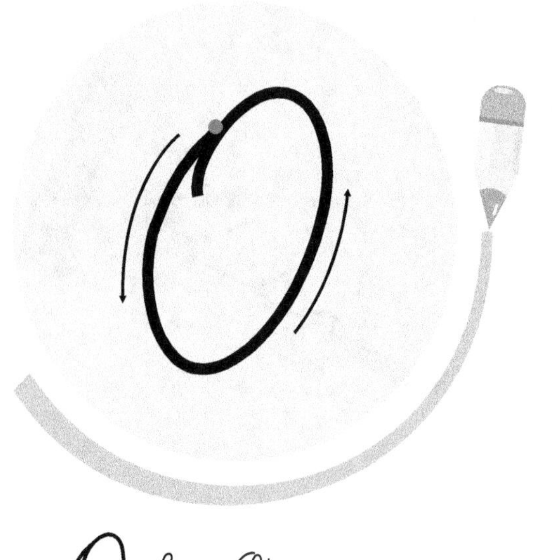

O for Orange

O O O O O O O O O O

O O O O O

O O O O

O O O

O O

O

Date: ....

Teacher's signature: ....

o for owl

Trace and write:

Date: ....

Teacher's signature: ....

P for Puppet

Trace and write:

(Cursive letter P tracing and writing practice rows)

Date: ....

Teacher's signature: ....

𝓅 for pup

Trace and write:

Date: ....

33

Teacher's signature: ....

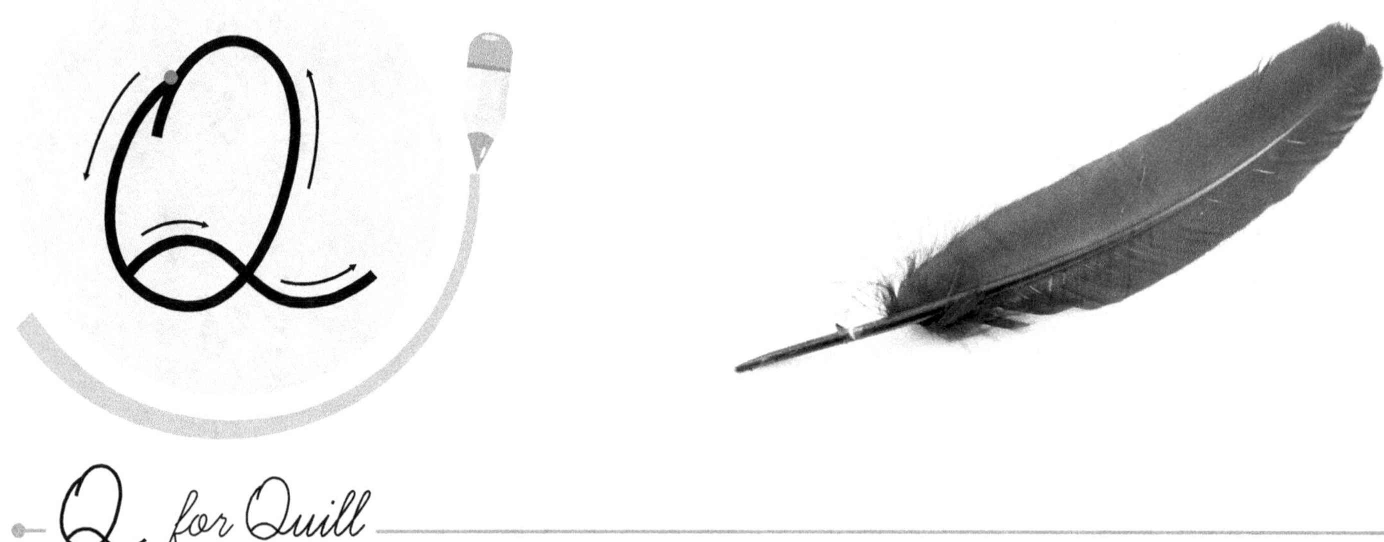

Q for Quill

Trace and write:

Date: ....

Teacher's signature: ....

q for quail

Date: .... 35 Teacher's signature: ....

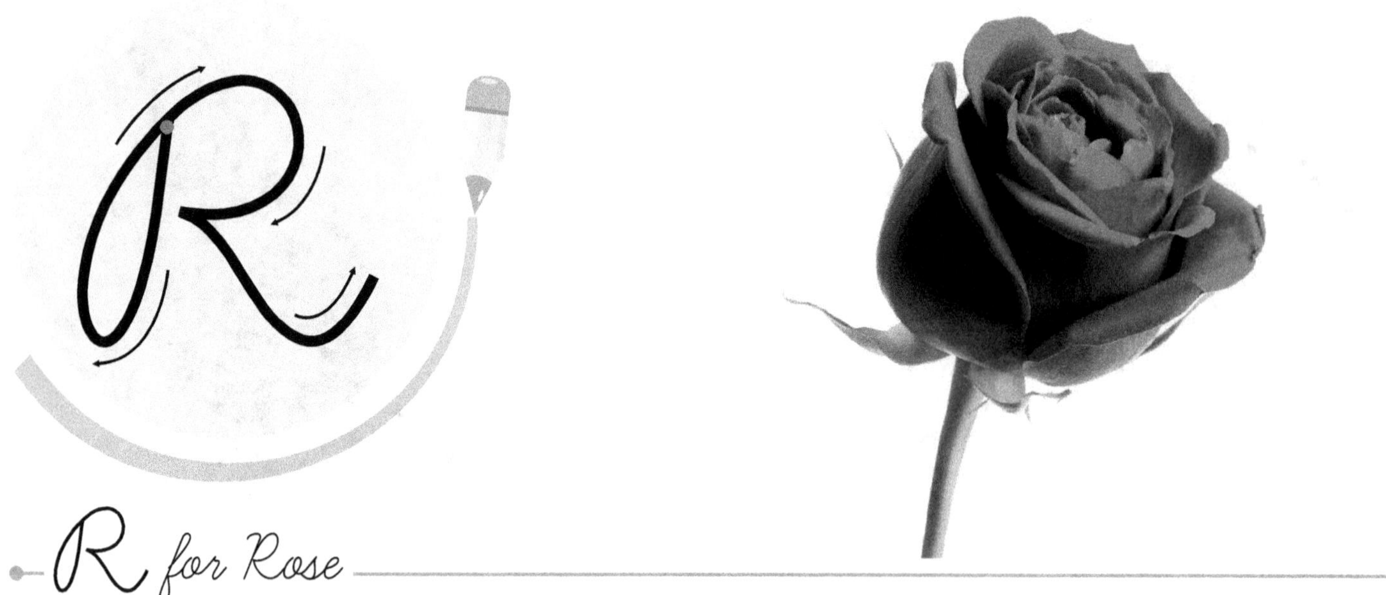

R for Rose

🦋 Trace and write:

R R R R R R R R R R R

R R R R R

R R R R

R R R

R R

R

Date: ....

Teacher's signature: ....

$\mathcal{r}$ for rabbit

$\mathscr{S}$ for Socks

👆 Trace and write:

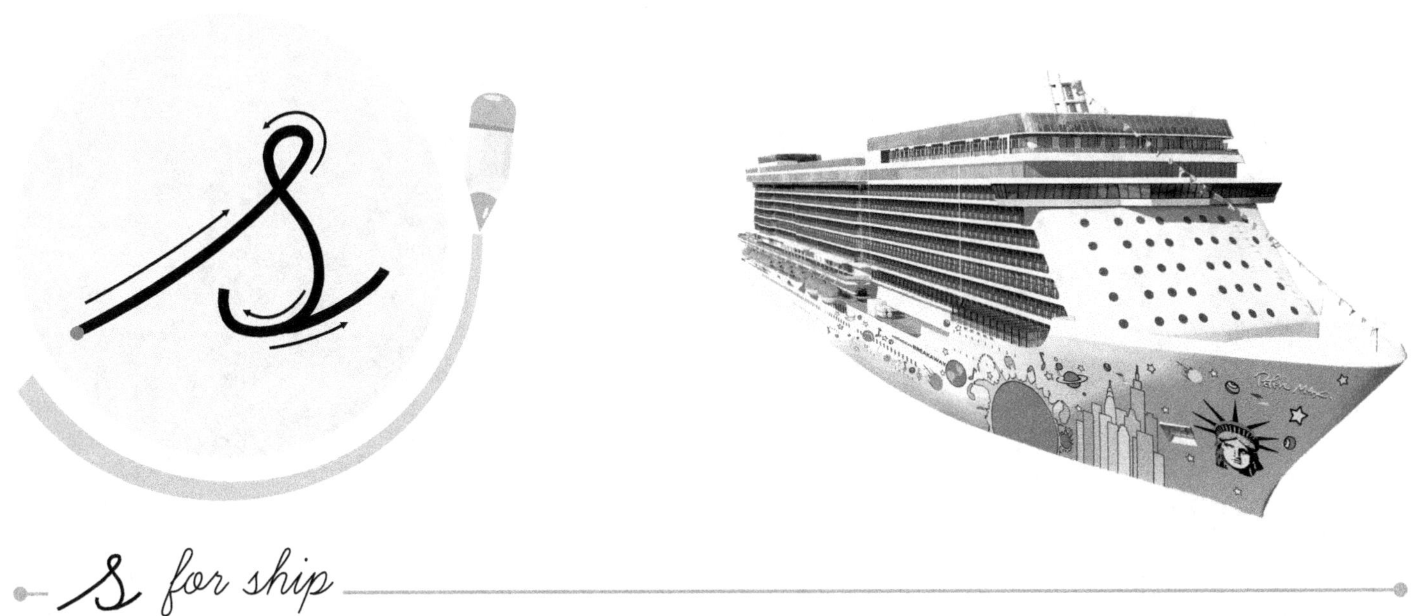

Trace and write:

Date: ....   Teacher's signature: ....

T for Top

Trace and write:

Date: .... 40 Teacher's signature: ....

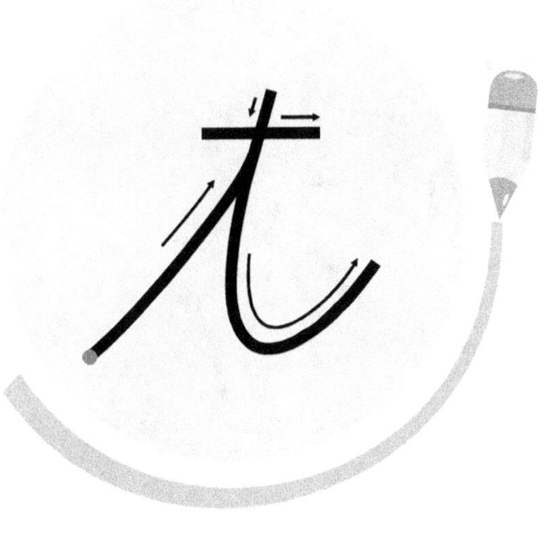

t for tiger

त त त त त त त त त त

त त त त त

त त त त

त त त

त त

त

Date: ....

Teacher's signature: ....

$\mathcal{U}$ *for Umbrella*

Trace and write:

Date: ....

Teacher's signature: ....

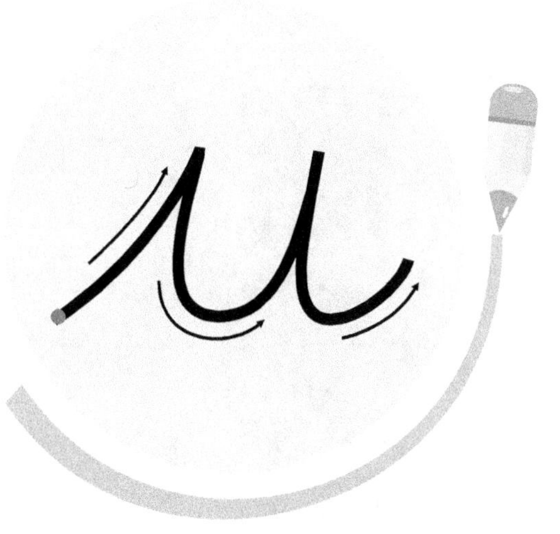

u for uniform

Trace and write:

Date: ....

Teacher's signature: ....

$\mathcal{V}$ for Vase

Trace and write:

Date: 44   Teacher's signature: ....

$\mathcal{V}$ for vegetables

Trace and write:

Date: 45   Teacher's signature: ....

W for Watch

Trace and write:

Date: ....

Teacher's signature: ....

w for watermelon

Trace and write:

Date: ....

Teacher's signature: ....

$\mathcal{X}$ *for Xmas tree*

🌸 Trace and write:

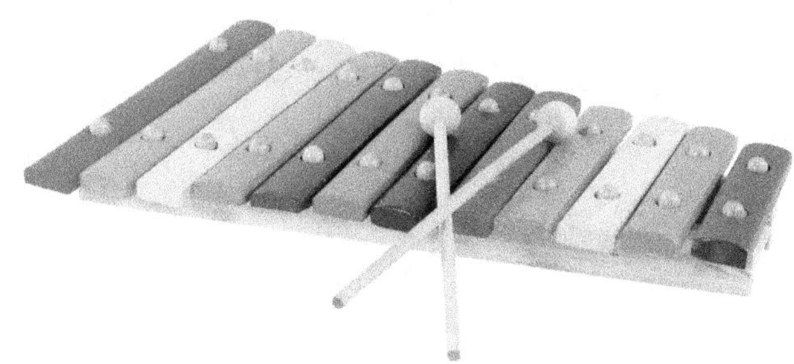

🖋 Trace and write:

Date: ....

Teacher's signature: ....

Y for Yo-Yo

🦋 Trace and write:

Y Y Y Y Y Y Y Y Y Y Y Y Y

Y Y Y Y Y Y Y

Y Y Y Y Y

Y Y Y

Y Y

Y

Y for yak

🖐 Trace and write:

$\mathscr{Z}$ for Zebra

🦋 Trace and write:

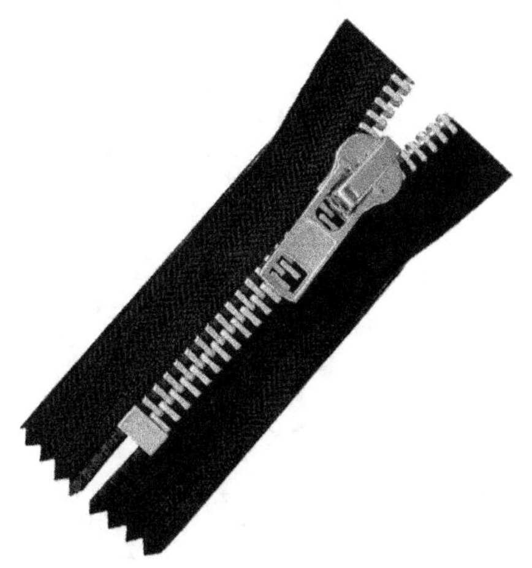

🐦 Trace and write:

Date: ....   Teacher's signature: ....

Date: ....

Teacher's signature: ....

🦋 Trace and write small letters:

| a | b | c | d | e | f | g | h |

| i | j | k | l | m | n | o | p |

| q | r | s | t | u | v | w | x |

| y | z |

🦋 Practice small letter a to z:

Date: ....   Teacher's signature: ....

Write the capital missing letters:

		C	D			G	
	J			N			
Q			T		V		

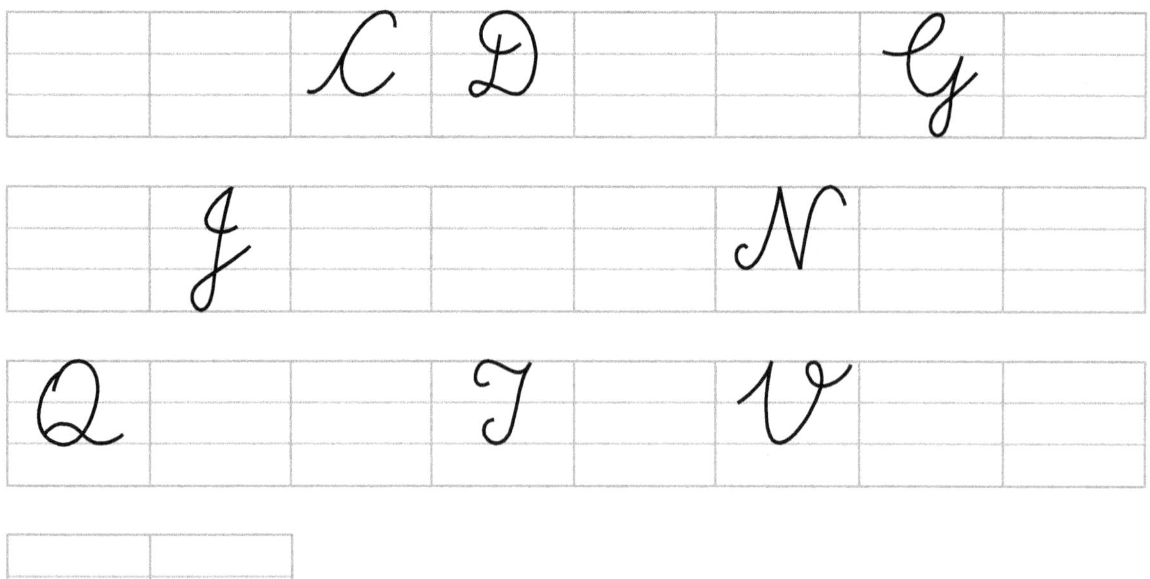

Write the small missing letters:

	b		e		g		
i			l		n		
r	s			v			
y							

www.ingramcontent.com/pod-product-compliance
Lightning Source LLC
LaVergne TN
LVHW082119190726
843495LV00012B/1707